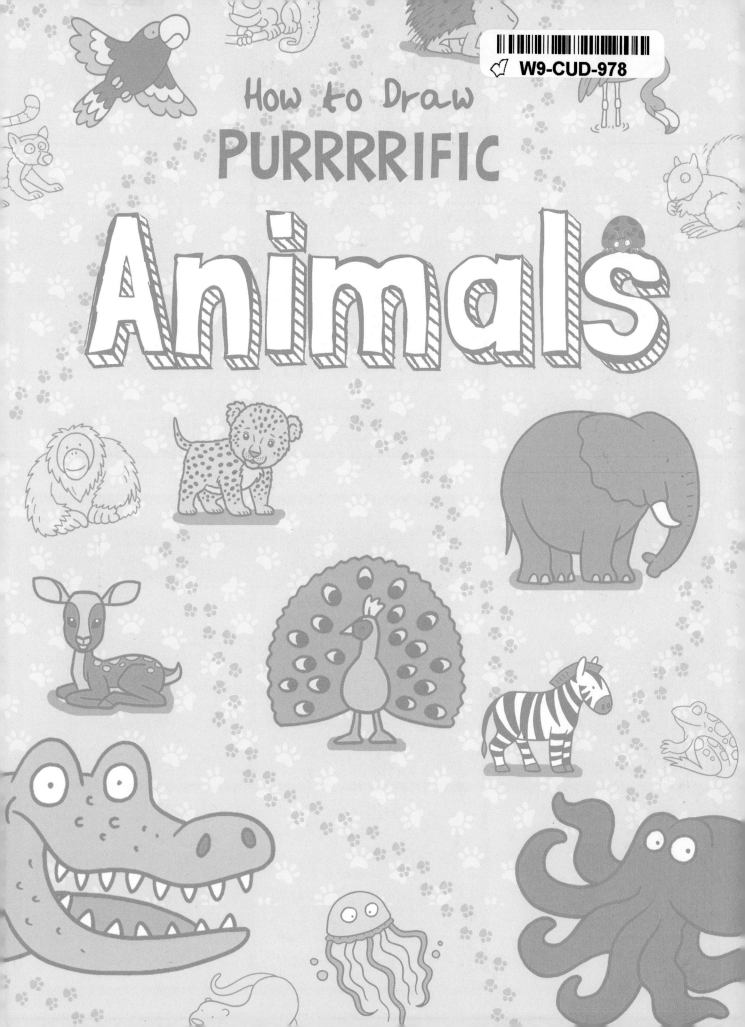

How to Draw
PURRRRIFIC
Animals

Lobster

Kangaroo

Eagle

Chimpanzee

Cat

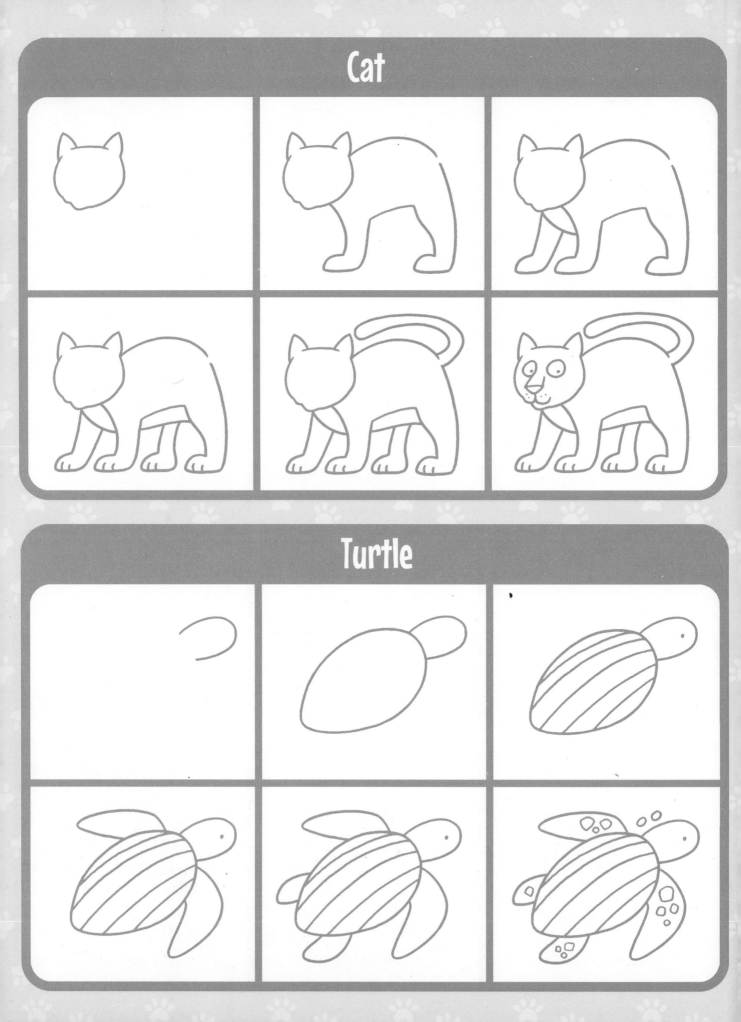

Turtle

Parrot

Stag Beetle

Budgie

Orang-utan

Rhino

Bat

Squirrel

Donkey

Toad

Owl

Crab

Dolphin

Peacock

Jellyfish

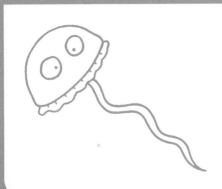  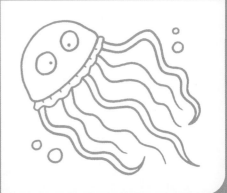

Otter

Zebra

Snail

Chameleon

Lemur

Bison

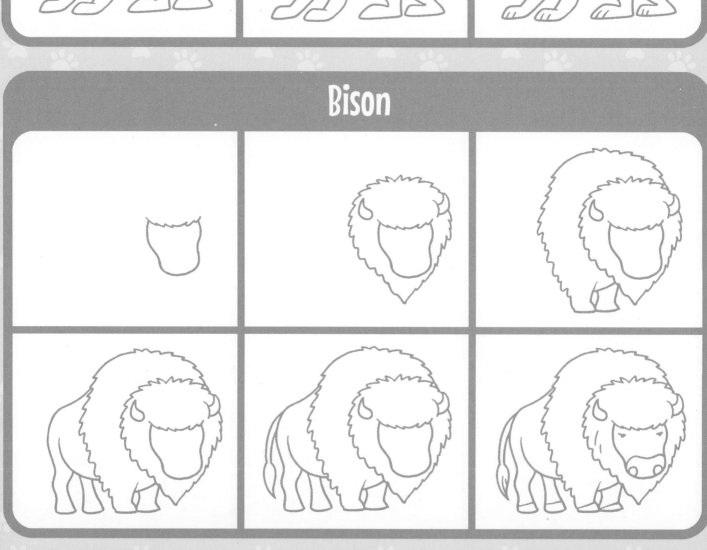

Elephant

Frog

Shark

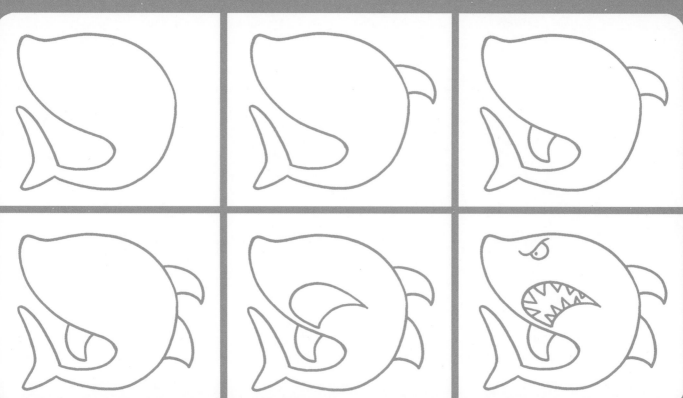

Goat

Duck

Porcupine

Spider

Mouse

Flamingo

Bear

Cheetah

Shrimp

Octopus

Ostrich

Cuttlefish

Ladybug

Orca

Crocodile

Mole

Wolf

Angler Fish

Woodpecker

House Fly

Hammerhead Shark

Bushbaby

Koala

Puppy

Kitten

Deer

Bear Cub

Calf

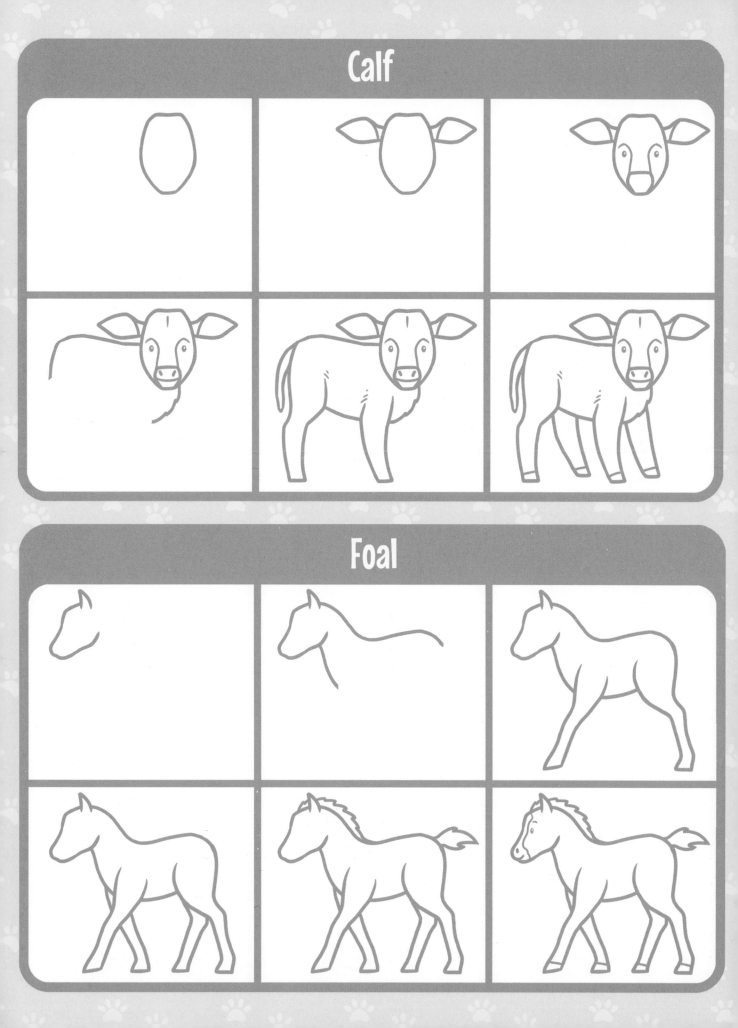

Foal

Panda

Penguin Chick

Seal Pup

Lamb

Leopard Cub

Cheetah Cub

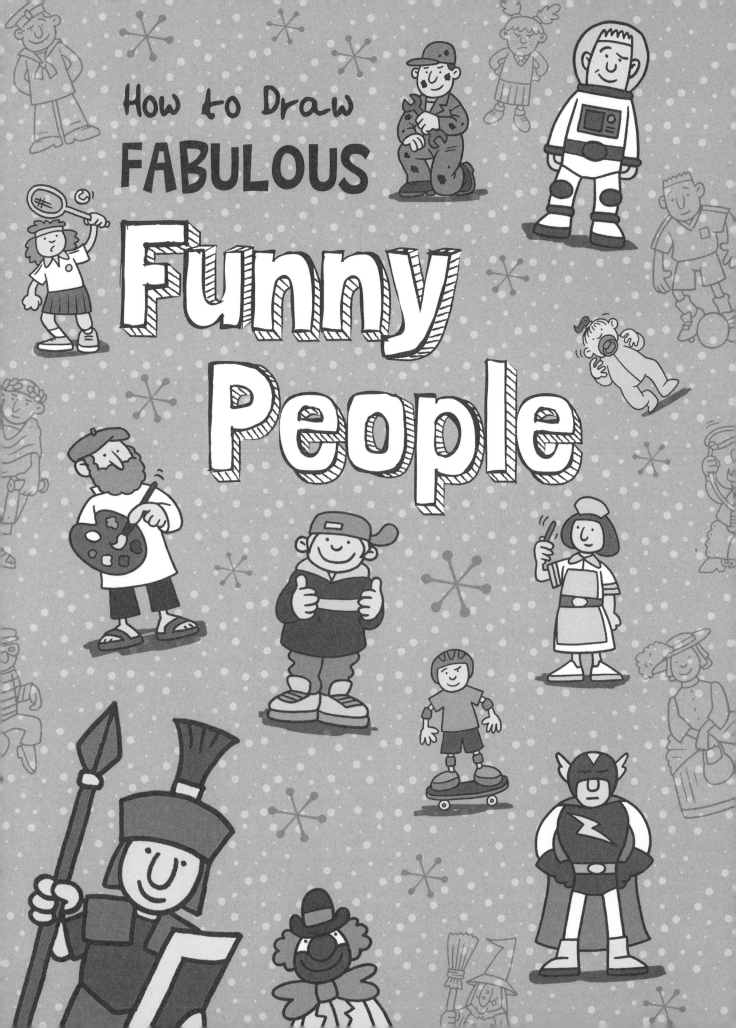

How to Draw
FABULOUS
Funny People

Roman Soldier

Baby

Roller Blades

Mechanic

Astronaut

School Girl

Astronaut

School Girl

King

Queen

Doctor

Musician

Woman

Man

Boy

Girl

Old Lady

Old Man

Pharaoh

Clown

Skateboarder

Greek Scholar

Cowboy

Flamenco Dancer

Infant

Judge

Greek Soldier

Old-fashioned Lady

Rock 'n' Roll Singer

Teacher

Black Belt

Sailor

Tennis Player

Construction Worker

Bride

Santa

Roman Emperor

Nurse

Opera Singer

Sheriff

Artist

Witch

Dentist

Soccer Player

Ice Skater

Superhero

Diver

Robber

Chef

Elf

Cave Woman

Cave Man

Gardener

Baseball Player

Fairy

Baker

Tightrope Walker

Fisherman

Magician

Knight

Security Guard

BMX

Happy Dancer

Mail Carrier

How to Draw
Really Cute
CHARACTERS

Princess Cutie Pie

Love Bunny

Moo Moo Cow

Little Bow Wow

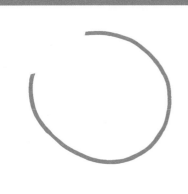

Unifaun

Pretty Kitty

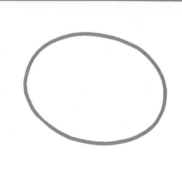  

Koal-ahh

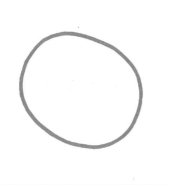  

Bubbles

Flick the Fairy

Chirpy

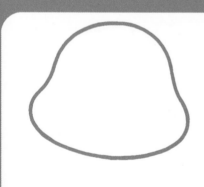

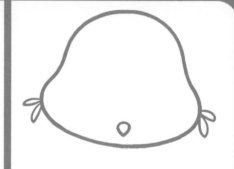

Munchkin

Bear Hug

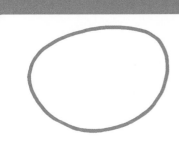 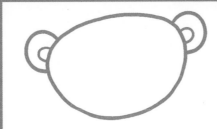 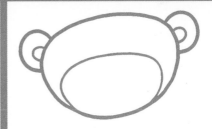

Poodle Pooch

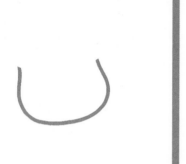

Fluffy

Puggle

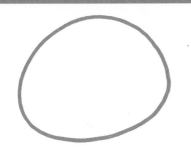 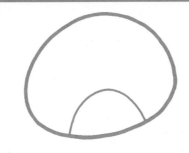 

Flame

Loxie

Dizzle

Trunky

Ickle Lion

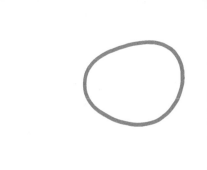

Puppy Love

Piggle

Sweetheart

Nibbles

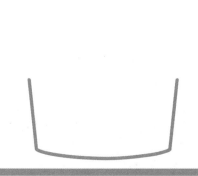  

Giggles

Pawpaw

Tiny

Pinkee

Sneezachoo

Tumtum

Snugglekins

Clopsy

Belle

Bluebell

Wiggly

Snowdrop

Waddles

Oinki

Tinky

Pandaisy

Splash

Tiddles

Bichon

Angel

Tangle

Groovy

Yodel

Bluey

Foxy

Tinchy

Tinchy Kimmi

Oo-la-la

Curly

Izzy

Baby Penguin

Unicorn

Daisy

Tizzle

Tickle

Wobble

Waffles

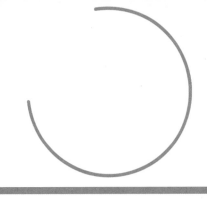

Snuffles

Lolly

Whirligig

Buzz

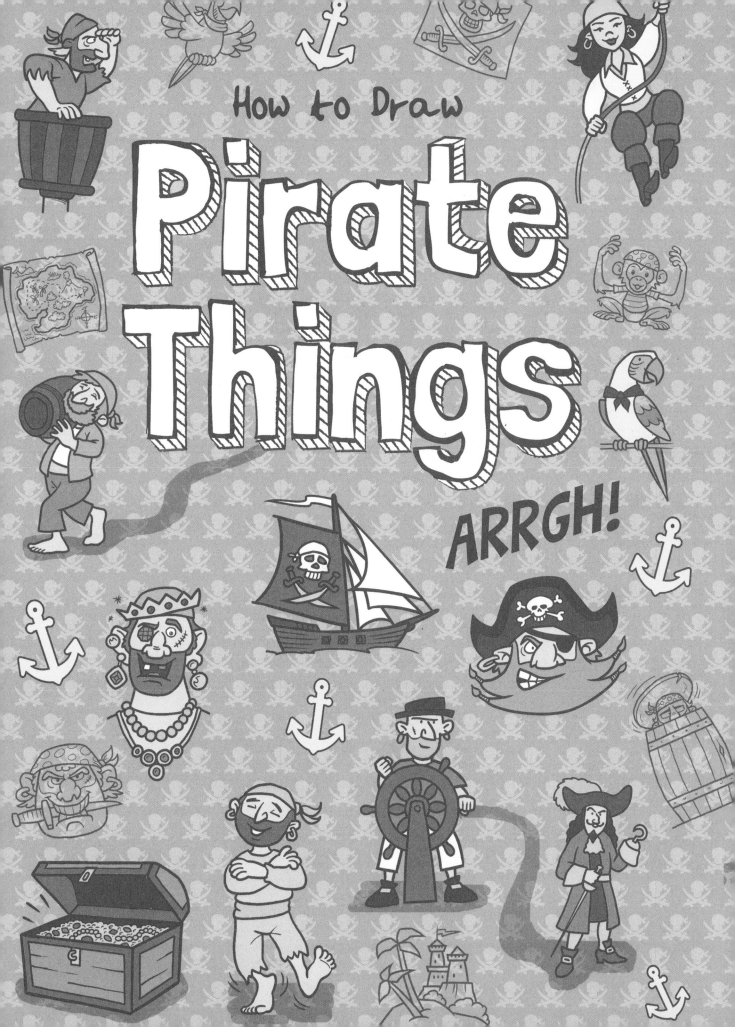

How to Draw

Pirate Things

ARRGH!

Blackbeard

Anne Bonny

Henry Morgan

Calico Jack

Mary Harvey

Black Bart

Sloop Ship

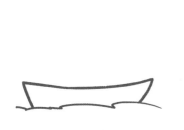
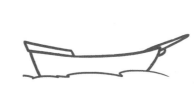

Treasure Chest

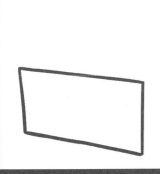
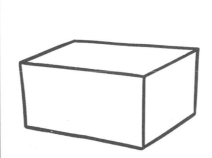

Calico Jack's Flag

 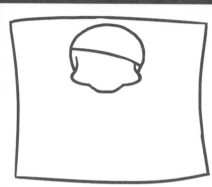 

Schooner Pirate Ship

Edward England

Captain Blood

Captain Hook

Jack Sparrow

Pirate Galleon

Island Fortress

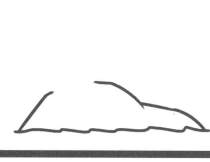

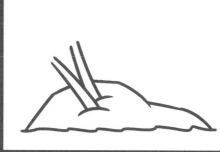

Treasure Map

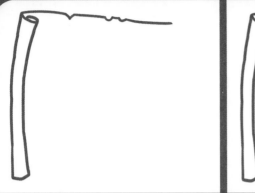  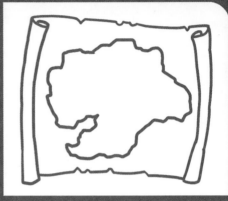

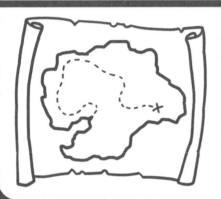  

Counting Treasure

Long John Silver

Polly

Sea Shanty

Pirate Jig

Swashbuckling Pirate

Cannonball Pete

Pirate with Cutlass

Cannon

 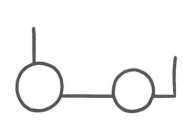 

Charging Pirate

Battered Pirate

Crow's Nest

Laughing Pirate

Big Ned

Cabin Boy

Climbing Pirate

Digging for Treasure

Mary Read

Climb the Rigging

Scared Pirate

Jumpy Pirate

Drinking Pirate

Pirate Firing Cannon

Fishing Pirate

Flying Parrot

Lazy Pirate

Nervous Pirate

Ship's Wheel

Pirate Stan

Jolly Roger

 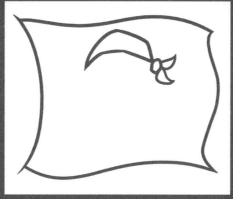 

Octopus

Pirate Head

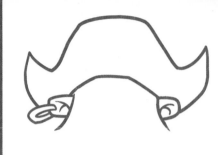
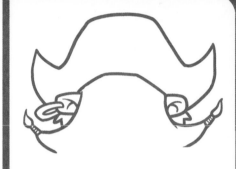
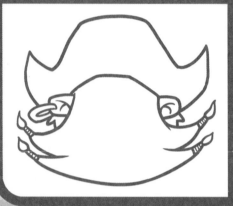

Pirate Eating

Pirate Hiding

Pirate Fiddler

Grace O'Malley

Pirate Bounty

Hauling the Sail

In the Brig

Mermaid Ahoy!

Pirate Monkey

Pirate with Barrel

Pirate with Lantern

Pirate with Map

Peg Leg Paul

How to Draw

Things That Go

1960s Racing Car

Viking Longship

Locomotive

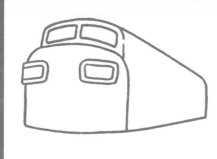

Spy Plane

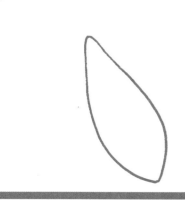

Formula 1 Racing Car

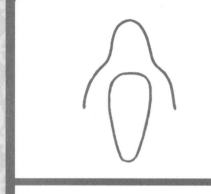 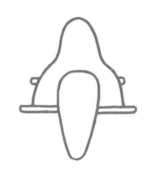 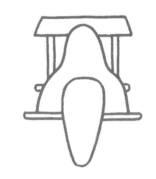

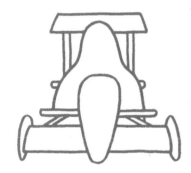 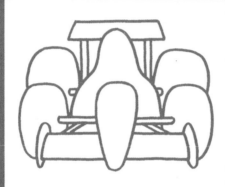 

Roadroller

Cruise Ship

Custom Bike

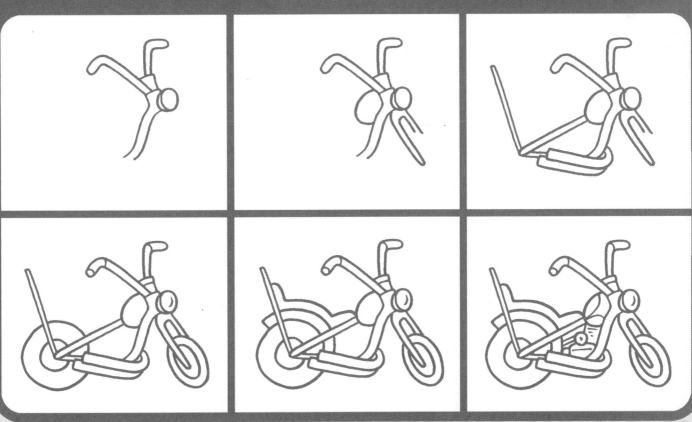

747 Jumbo Jet

Custom Car

Micro Car

Digger

Rescue Patrol Boat

Helicopter

Snowmobile

Moon Buggy

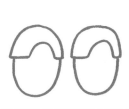  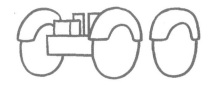

Crane

High Speed Locomotive

Combine Harvester

Racing Motorbike

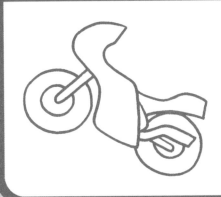

Squad Car

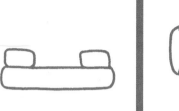

Wright Brothers' Flyer

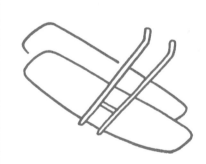

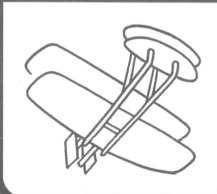

Mini Digger

Jet Ski

Space Shuttle

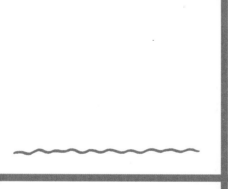

Junk Ship

Off-Roader

Bullet Train

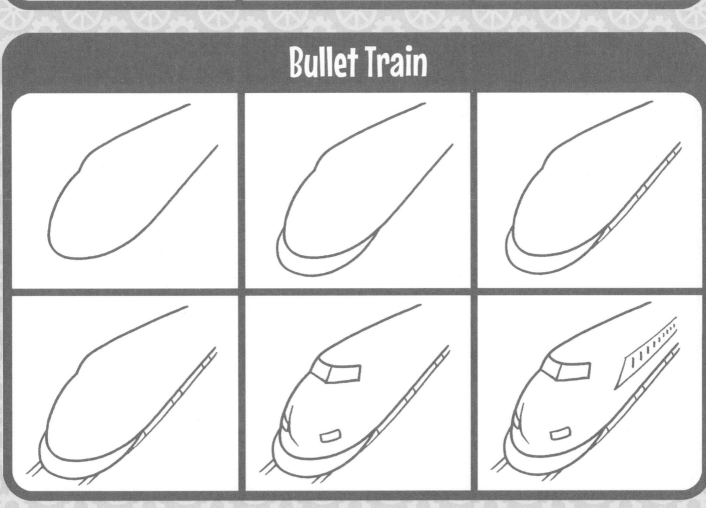

Motorbike

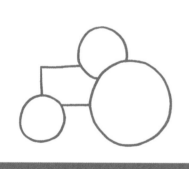

Traction Engine

Stealth Fighter

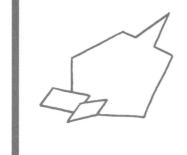

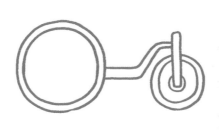
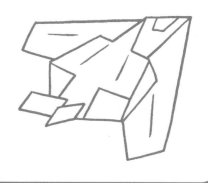

The First Car

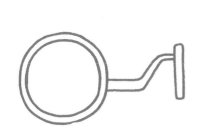

Mini Dump Truck

Cadillac

Motorized Rickshaw

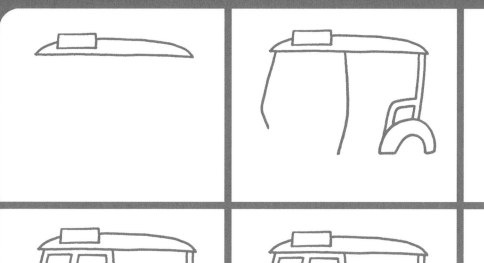

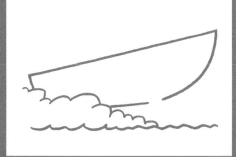

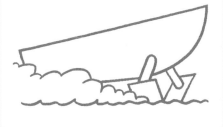

Hydrofoil

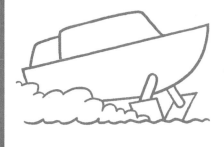

Railroad Snowplow

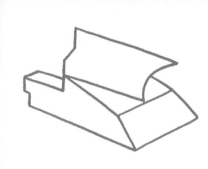
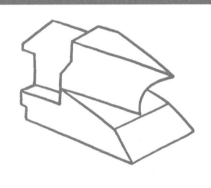

Spitfire

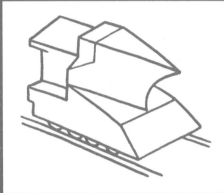

Bubble Car

 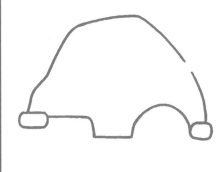 

Cement Truck

Ultralight

Paddle Steamer

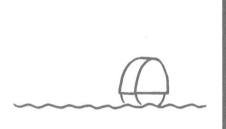
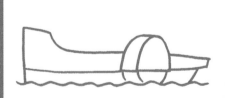

17th Century Ship

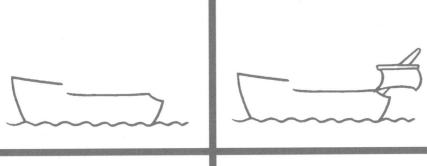

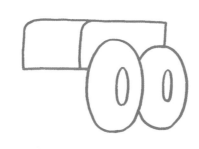

Monster Truck

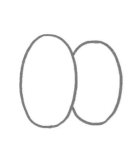

Dump Truck

Scooter

Le Mans Racing Car

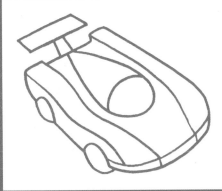

Dumpster Truck

Hovercraft

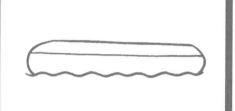  

  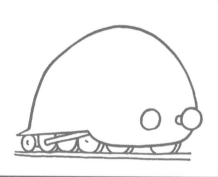

The Mallard Steam Locomotive

 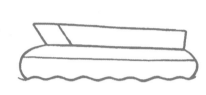 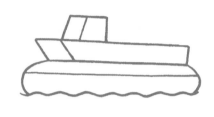

Mini Roller

Fishing Boat

Pick-up Truck

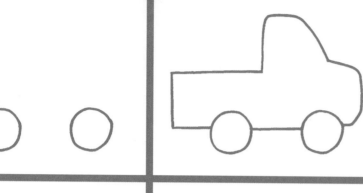

Freight Truck

Speedboat

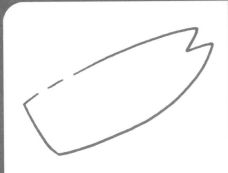

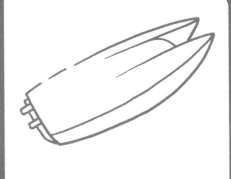

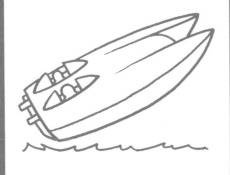

1901 Oldsmobile

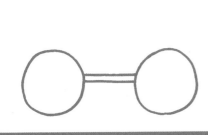

Seaplane

London Bus

 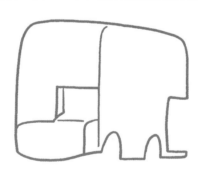 

Bulldozer

Sports Utility Vehicle

Rolls Royce

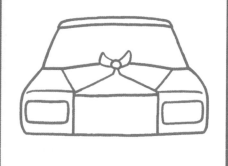

Light Airplane

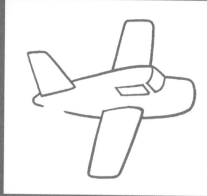

How to Draw
BEAUTIFUL
Horses
and Ponies

Arab

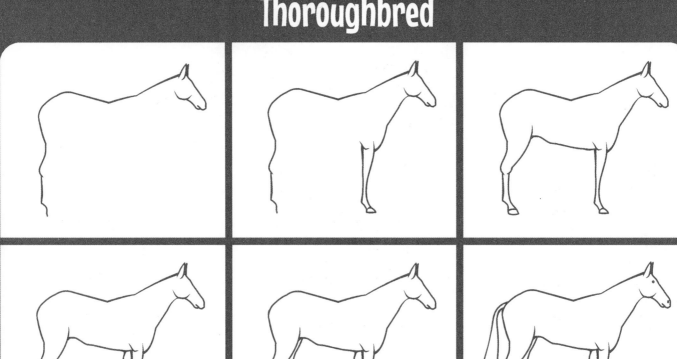

Thoroughbred

Horse Over Stable Door

Horses With Nose Markings

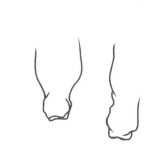

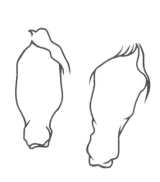

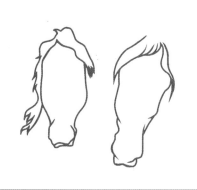

Friesian

Dartmoor

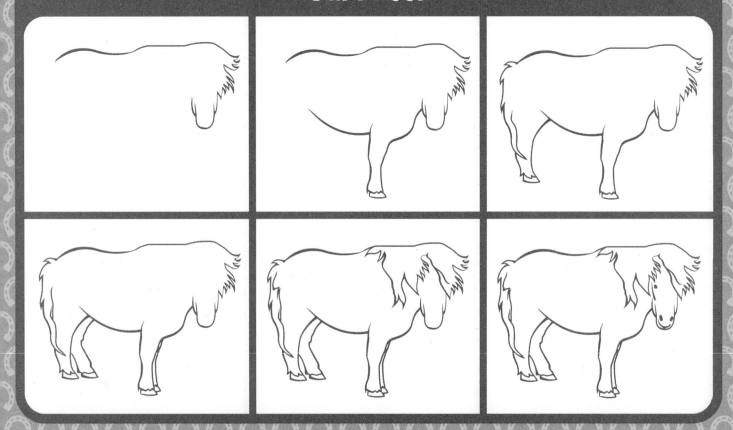

Lusitano

Lipizzaner

Mustang

Piebald

Shire

Falabella

Appaloosa

Shetland Pony

Palomino

Norwegian Fjord Pony

Breton

Pinto

Walking

Trotting

Cantering

Galloping

Jumping

Eating Grass

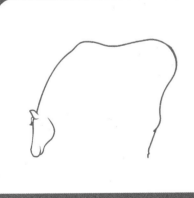

Rearing

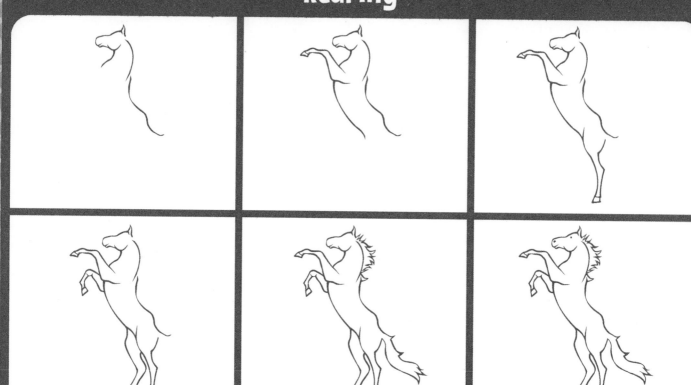

Tethered

Circus Horse

Whinnying

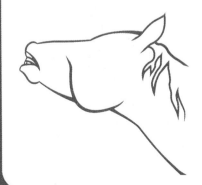  

Prehistoric Horse

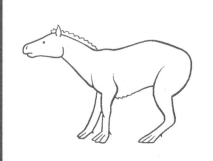
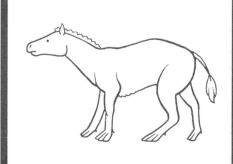

Horse And Rosette

Dressage Horse

Bridled Horse

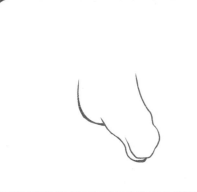

Bucking Bronco With Rider

Polo Pony With Rider

Mother And Foal

Racehorse With Blinkers

Medieval Tournament Horse

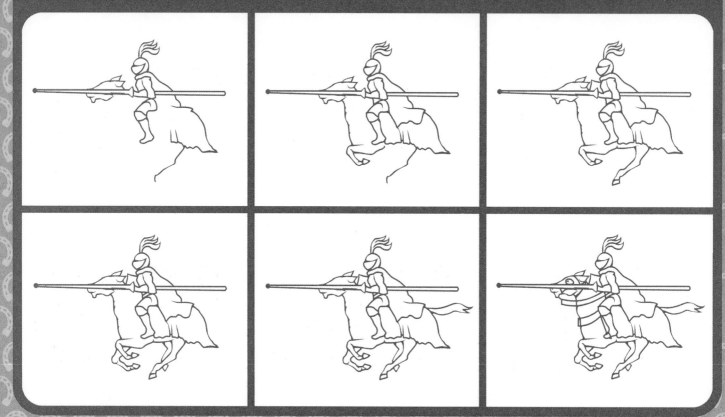

Expression; Ears Forward

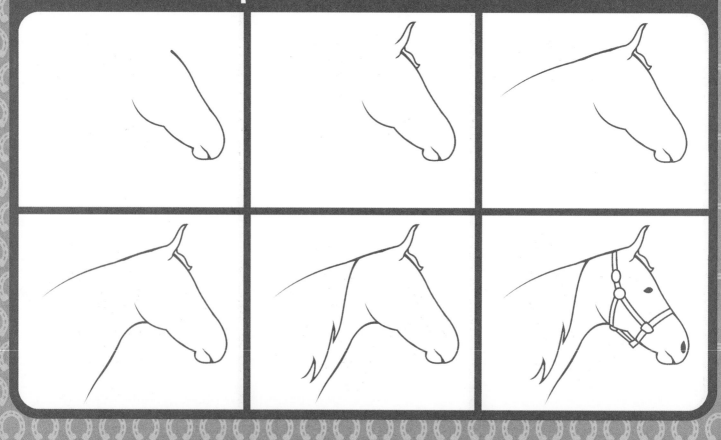

Expression: Ears Back

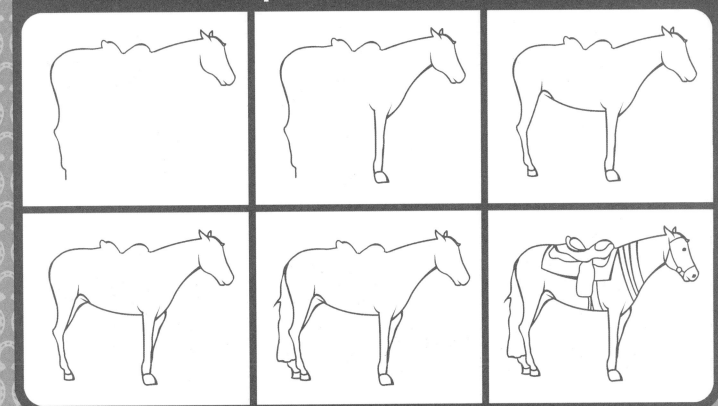

Harness Racing

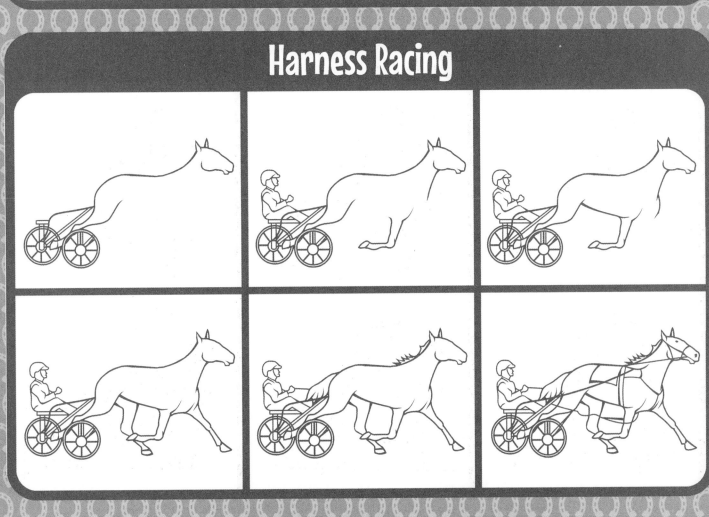

Classical Equitation

Eventing Horse

Two Heads Nuzzling

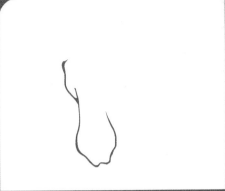 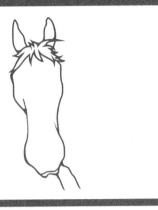 

  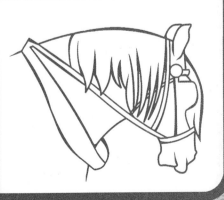

Show Horse

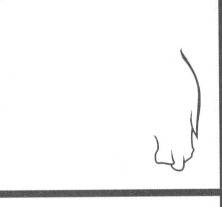 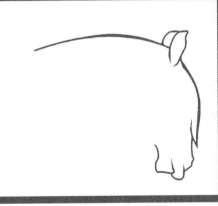 

 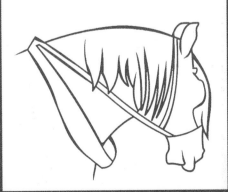 

Mustang Close-Up

Thoroughbred Close-Up

Piebald Pony

Eating Hay

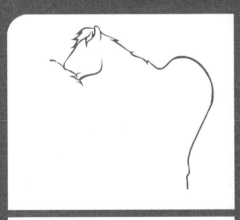  

Plaited Tail

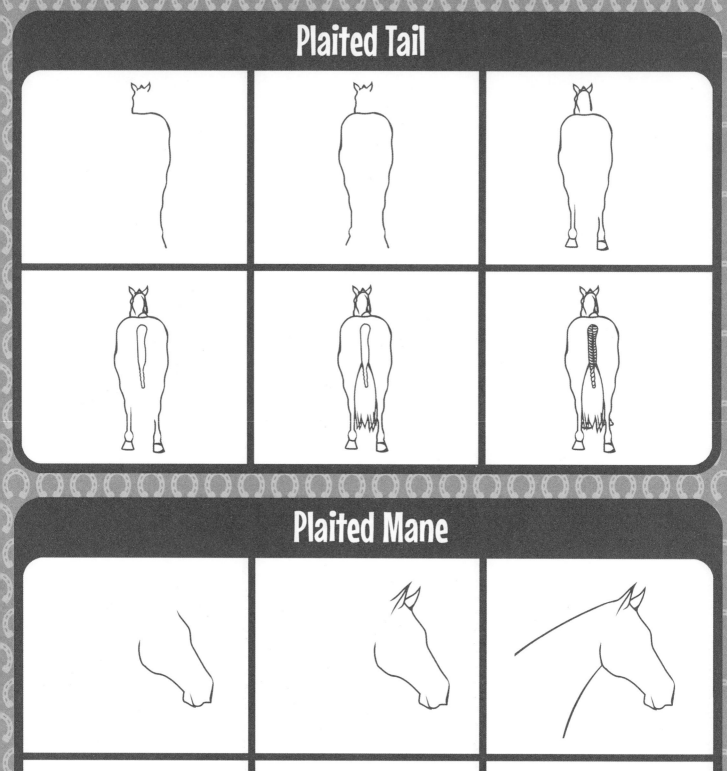

Plaited Mane

Horse In Horsebox

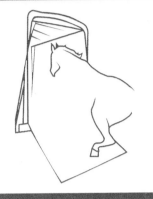  

 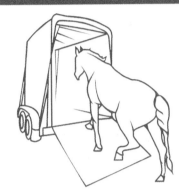 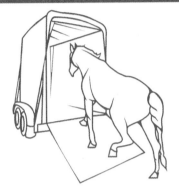

Rear View Of Saddle

Horse Lying Down

Horse Rolling Over

Horse Pawing The Ground

Horse With Blanket

Foal

Horse Being Re-Shod

Horse Led With a Halter

Police Horse

Jockey On Horse

Canadian Mountie Horse

Snarf

Borgle

Clopsy

Mutant

Marsian

Starship Trooper

Amoeboid

Rocket

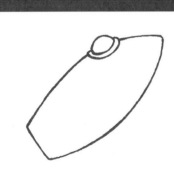
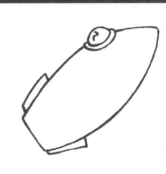

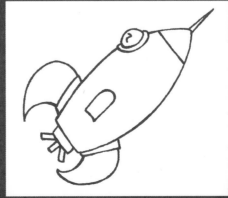

Predator

Flying Saucer

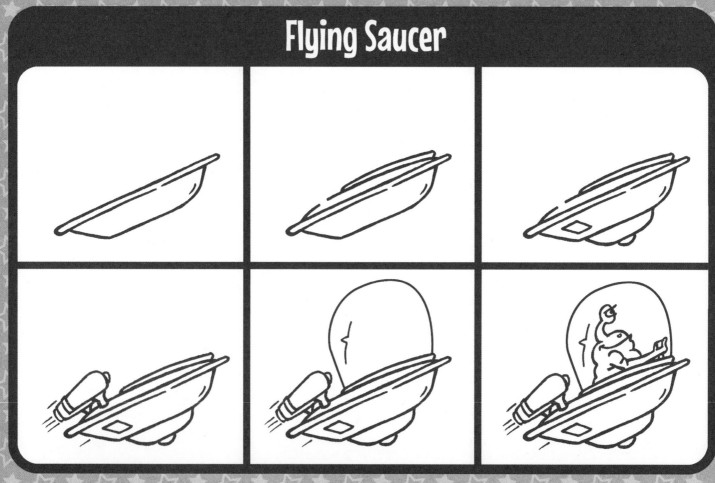

Delta

Zakbar

Big Banger

Gobble

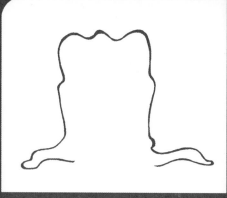  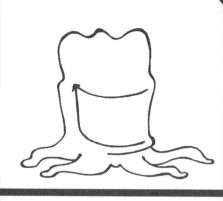

Zoom

Battle Droid

Asteroidus

Jabber

Lightspeed

Neutreno

Laser

Worker Droid

Space Monkey

Fisheye

Spaced Out

Impact

Meteorus

Lunar

Astronaut

Elkan

Pluton

Alien X

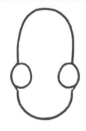
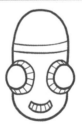

Electro

Nebulus

Starship Destroyer

Space Pirate

Gravitoid

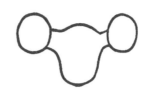 

Warp

Space Dog

Bugle

Apocalypse

Mollusk

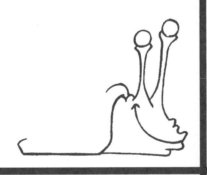
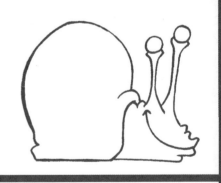

Arachnid

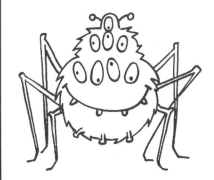

Beagle

Blaster

Bounty Hunter

Zap

Starcrawler

Rocket Witch

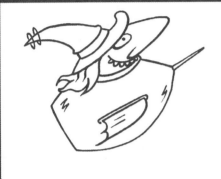  

Planeteer

Moondusa

Moonpig

Matrix

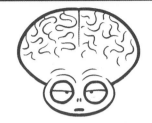

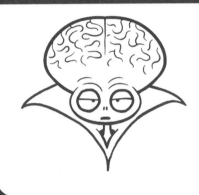
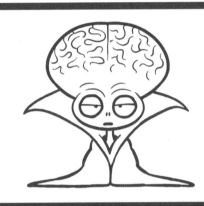

Infantry Droid

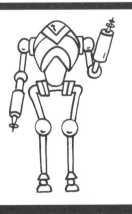

Nemotoad

Ice Planet Trooper

Star Man

Plasma

Space Troll

Alien Medic

Space Raider

Optimus

Neptunus

Space Sumo

Red Planet Beast

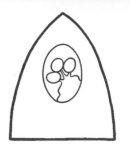

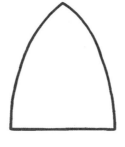

Fraggle

How to Draw
SUPER COOL
Manga

Ponytail

Young Girl

Teddy Cuddle

Happy Girl

School Girl

Trendy Girl

Catsuit

Skipping

Dancing

Cool Girl

Sleepyhead

Curly Hair

Thumbs Up

Annoyed

Laid Back

Shy Girl

Braids

School Boy

Soccer Player

Angry Boy

Grumpy Boy

Relaxed

Trendy Boy

Cool Boy

Smart Boy

Waving

Cookies

Yo-Yo

Attitude

Skater

Shy Boy

Bandana

Hoody

Ready to Go

Magical Woman

Business Woman

Dancer

Athletic Woman

Racer

Walker

Karate Girl

Japanese Lady

Psychic

Winter Woman

Mother

Archer

Smart Lady

Party Woman

Smart Guy

Relaxed Dude

Karate

Runner

Arms Folded

Elf Archer

Leader

Cool Dude

Rocker

Robot